DRAGON VALOUR

By

Serena Scarlett

Dragon Valour - a novella
by Serena Scarlett
Published by Om Purity P/L

Also by Serena Scarlett
The Autistic Dragon
Bardin & The Hob Folke
Get Published: Industry Experts Share Their Secrets

DRAGON

VALOUR

Author Serena Scarlett
Prologue by Serena Scarlett
Editors Steve Pye & Roger Feltham

Published Om Purity Pty Ltd

ISBN 978-0-6456386-5-3

The knights of Belongh, much like the legendary Knights Templar, were steeped in a rich history of valiant service and protection. Being medieval and somewhat akin to 14th Century Earthland years, their style was one of honour and valour.

Despite their formidable martial prowess and readiness to defend those under their care, they were renowned for their commitment to peace, in an age where warfare had become a distant memory.

The Belonghi knights were known for their gentleness and unwavering dedication to safeguarding their homeland and its inhabitants. Many of them flew on bonded dragons.

Peace and security reigned over the land. There was a natural, longstanding hierarchy. Many among the Belonghi were of high repute, being direct ancestors of the original knights. A number of them had dragons that they were bonded with from a young age.

Massive, fire-breathing, but otherwise gentle creatures. For the most part the dragons were taken for flights across the island to inspect crops or to visit far-flung parishes. When needed their fire, speed and strength were occasionally used in battle. Battles that for the most part were now only re-enactments.

The heads of the household in the village of Ridgecliff had lived long and productive lives, farming and raising a family of four bold children who had flourished under their care. Two boys and two girls had grown under chivalrous values and learnt the importance of being of service and contribution to community. Their parents, who had held strong moral codes and traditions, had lived healthily as crop and vegetable farmers to a very old age.

Now orphans, the four were direct descendants of the revered Belonghi knights. The two sons had dragons they were imprinted by and they could often be seen flying together over farming lands and along the coast.

The family's village was situated on the large island of Chasinghi. Their family homestead overlooked the sea bordered by high cliffs. The homestead was situated on a plateau of arable farming land, edged by tall trees.

Chapter 1

The climb up the cliff required concentration but was not hard. Sitting down on a smooth rock halfway up the steep incline, Jazintu noticed a dark shadow indicating a small cave entrance. It wasn't far above her so by carefully clambering over a few rocky outcrops she was close enough to view it better.

Leaning around to look in she was met with two golden glowing orbs looking straight back at her.
Startled but not scared, Jazintu moved her body to face the entrance directly. An animal was living in there, "I wonder what it is," she mused. Edging closer, at the same time making gentle cooing noises, she hoped she sounded mothering or caring.

The eyes closed slightly like a cat's when smiling. Reassured by this Jazintu entered the cave, the entrance curving just above her head. The creature rustled as it slid back a little and opened its eyes wider as Jazintu blocked the light from the entrance.

Orbs of gold with an emerald-green centre regarded her and Jazintu talked in a soft voice with the hope of continuing the connection.

"Hello, beauty, nice to meet you magickal one."

She sat in the dusty entrance, and turned side-on to the creature. This gave both of them a view out of the cave and she was no longer blocking the exit for the young dragon.

A young dragon is what she had discovered. She had heard tales of large ones in outer rural parishes that were magnificent fire-breathing beasts that blackened the sky when they flew in front of the Sun. The stories of those giants told how they were the enemy. Whereas locally the wild gentle smaller dragons still occasionally flew over her family's farm. Some had riders, some flew solo. Jazintu wasn't sure which breed this one was.

Now that her eyes had adjusted to the dimmer light of the cave Jazintu could make out the scaly shape of soft leathery skin. There was a hint of dark emerald-green on its sides and a silvery shine on her short scaly tail.

The green and silver glowed slightly like crystals in the light, but a glow was also emanating from within the skin. Jazintu considered the dragon to be female as they tended to have a translucent glow through their skin.

Suddenly the little dragon shot forward and the colours became electric, the silver and green flashing as bright as her eyes. As the dragon slid to a stop, only a hand's width from her side, Jazintu could feel the warmth of the baby dragon's breath on her leg. Before she could reach out to touch the dragon, a screech rang out across the water.

Still hidden from sight, Jazintu looked out. The dragon's mother had returned and was flying towards the cave. The massive beauty appeared to be injured as one wing hung lower and her flight was uneven.

Unsure of the mother's protective fierceness, Jazintu scrambled out and swung around the corner, out of sight from the cave entry.

Staying still, almost holding her breath, she waited.

Landing above her, the dragon mother perched on a craggy rock and leaning forward put her muzzle into the cave's entry.

Jazintu, still mostly hidden, could see the powerful body, a deep red-maroon, and her huge clawed legs with dark brown scales at her thighs and shining outer scales flashing black and red as she moved.
Burping and belching out came fish and water. Food for her young, some chewed, some whole but fresh and plenty of it spewed into the entrance for the baby dragon. Rather than instantly pouncing onto the seeping mass, it poked at it curiously, sniffing and nibbling.

Then, off she went, the mother dragon winding down the cliff face in one long spinning sweep. Jazintu could make out what appeared to be a burn and a gaping gash down one side of her flanks. Then the dragon was out of sight as she turned and spun away.
Jazintu retraced her steps and entered the cave once more. She watched from just inside as the baby dragon

ate its fill. The way the dragon ate was curious. It would first sniff, lick then nibble each piece before taking a full bite. Then, as if delighted with the taste, it would make happy sounds after chewing and swallowing each morsel.

Having been totally absorbed in dining, the dragon appeared to have forgotten Jazintu's presence. It looked up finally and smiled with its eyes, half closing them in contentment. The dragon shuffled towards Jazintu and this time she took the opportunity of the dragon's close proximity. She slowly reached forward and stroked the side of the dragon. Immediately cooing sounds were emitted. Encouraged, Jazintu stroked further, moving her hand over the back and then around the small head.

Jazintu moved around the whole dragon gently exploring the whole body, stroking and speaking gently. "Hello you beautiful, baby dragon, magickal You." Coos were issued in reply. Jazintu resumed her position at the front of the dragon and they gazed into each other's eyes. Both mesmerized, a bond of mutual admiration and love forming.

She marvelled at its size and agility. She estimated that being a third of a fully grown one, it was not gangly at all and was easily able to manoeuvre in the small cave.

Jazintu knew of others that had been imprinted by baby dragons. Theirs had been from a formal ritual that occurred when an elder passed away and, as one dragon and rider left, new dragons emerged to take their place. She hadn't ever heard of a bonding like this, by a chance meeting.

However, she knew enough that this dragon would now be 'hers'. Once a meal had been eaten in the presence of their person and petting allowed, the bonding consummated. The irrefutable spiritual connection was formed and nothing could break the imprint. Concerned the mother would return again and not look kindly on her presence, Jazintu reluctantly decided to leave and return another time.

Chapter 2

Jazintu climbed the short few stone steps to the top of the cliff, taking the last ones in light leaps.
She was now back on the plateau not far from the family home. Her morning walk had taken her on a circular route. A gentle but long path led to the beach and, enjoying the physical exertion, Jazintu had climbed the cliff on her way back.

Thrilled with her find and wanting to share the news she ran across the flat ground of the plateau. It wasn't until she could see the front door of the homestead that she slowed to catch her breath.

What would she say? Should she tell her brothers, Jasper and Mordan or should she just confide in her older sister, Lazura who she usually shared everything with?
Not her brothers, she concluded. They would tell too many others and besides the young dragon was her

secret, her special story, not one for the whole community. Not yet.

And Lazura? She could trust her, but she would want to come and see the little dragon and for now, Jazintu wanted to visit alone, and bond further.
Perhaps she would keep it totally secret. For now.
Bonding with dragons was the best part. She'd heard of it and been intrigued by the way two-legged humans and four-legged winged beings could become as one. Feelings and emotions were transmitted by a kind of telepathic energy passing between each other.

Sitting for a while to compose herself, Jazintu closed her eyes and imagined the young dragon, her shining golden eyes and elegant form curled up in the cave.
She felt a surge of emotions, love and a type of maternal pride. Feeling her soft arms embracing the little one, her cheek resting against its soft leathery cheek. The warm gentle air of her breath tickling her nose. She wondered what its name was. Then it came to her, Jazintu spoke the name "Emeraldesa."

"Eeep, Eeep zeep zeep, Ziip," the reply came instantly. Looking around Jazintu realised it wasn't nearby, although it sounded clear. It was inside but outside her. Inside her mind, not in her proximity, but still heard by her ears.

An image came to her, the little dragon's eyes golden looking straight into hers and a more gentle "eeep"

"Eeep," she cooed in reply.

"Wow, it's already started," Jazintu mused. The bonding was deepening. She felt a warm tingle and a pull on her heart strings.

Amazed that she could hear and feel the dragon at such a distance from the cave, Jazintu knew this was a rare and magickal experience.

Initially she thought she was simply imagining the dragon, but in fact, when she could see the dragon in her mind's eye, she was actually doing so. The dragon had formed a connection and was communicating with her.

Her mind raced forward. A life with a dragon. Would it be by her side all day, sleep at the foot of her bed at night? Her room was so small, she may have to move into the barn!

Determined to plan a habitable space, Jazintu headed straight home and into the barn to check its suitability. With her ageing family the farm had been less productive for many years. Even when her father was alive he had rarely used the outbuildings. Her brothers had simpler duties nowadays, managing the goats and cattle and occasional rotation crops.

Jazintu considered the disused barn that was rarely visited by anyone as a good hiding place. It would be ideal for when the dragon was ready to move in. The barn was a long distance from the homestead being an old hay storage shed near crumbling ruins. No-one ventured there anymore. As children, they had played among the rubble of the now inhabitable dwelling. She made her way through the scrub and rocky ground to reach the hidden location.

As she pushed open the large wooden doors, light shone on the dust raised from the old hay. No longer being used to store feed, the barn was empty except for some loose straw, crates, wooden chests and a few farming tools.

Climbing the stairs at the back of the barn, Jazintu peered around at the large space and decided it could be a perfect loft bedroom for her dragon.

Noticing that the barn needed a sweep, she cleaned the space and noted what she would need to bring such as water bowls and fresh straw for bedding.

Now to find Lazura. Unable to contain her excitement, she was considering telling her sister after all. Walking quickly, almost running, she made her way across the yard, along the garden path that led to the back door. She could see one of her brothers cooking and the other grabbing at food and they were both hitting each other in jest.

To avoid them she took a wide berth to the side entrance and raced upstairs to the bedrooms. Jazintu found

Lazura in the room next to hers at her easel absorbed in her drawing. She was sketching healing remedies of herbs and flowers that their late mother had taught them to use. Lazura was making a record of them as a reference for herself and others.

Plumping herself down next to her sister, Jazintu took a deep breath. "You are not going to believe what I have found!" Lazura turned to her sister, her blue penetrating eyes inviting more.

"I have found a cave with a ..." Before she could finish her brothers Jasper and Mordan bounded into the room. They had a plate of freshly baked biscuits and all four of them took several and began to eat.

Lazura, aged in her late twenties, was the oldest of the siblings. Jazintu the youngest was now eighteen. Mordan and Jasper, aged a year apart, were in their mid-twenties.

Enjoying the wholesome snack, the brothers admired the room, commenting on each drawing.

Having lost the moment, Jazintu didn't tell her sister after all. Lazura then resumed her drawing and Jazintu decided not to disturb her further.

Going to her own room she planned what she could start taking to the barn to make it comfortable for when the time came for Emeraldesa to move in. If indeed that was what would happen. She didn't really know, but she wanted to be prepared if it turned out that the dragon's mother had died. The older dragon had certainly been badly injured when Jazintu had seen her flying near the cliffs where she first found Emeraldesa.

Armed with sturdy bowls, a thin mattress and a change of clothing, she made her way back to the barn. As she entered, she looked up to the loft and for a moment she thought she saw two golden orbs again. Were they dragon eyes looking at her out of the dim room? Yes, there it was again, the gold and green glow. The dragon baby was already there! It had taken itself there. Jazintu pondered if the young one had followed her scent to the farm and inside the barn.

Chapter 3

Jazintu returned to the homestead and raided the kitchen pantry. She chose what foods she imagined a dragon may eat and soon found she had guessed correctly.

She visited Emeraldesa daily and fed warm goat's milk, honey and ground meat to the eager dragon. Each morning, before dawn, the sounds of pleasure came moments before she opened the barn door.

The young dragon was a delightful creature with shiny scales and eyes that sparkled with curiosity. Emeraldesa's senses were keen, and she seemed to anticipate Jazintu's arrival each day. Even before the barn door creaked open, the air would be filled with the soft rustle of wings and an excited chittering sound. The baby dragon was enthusiastically welcoming, evident in the way its tail twitched and its wings quivered in excitement.

As Jazintu stepped into the barn, the dragon's joy became even more apparent. The clinking of the tray and the familiar scents of its favourite treats would elicit a series of delighted sounds from the dragon.

With each morsel of goat's milk-soaked bread, each taste of honey, and every bite of the tender meatballs, the dragon's pleasure was evident. It would emit excited squeaks.

Nurtured through these daily rituals of nourishment and companionship, the bond between caretaker and dragon was deepening. And as the dragon continued to grow, so did the strength of this bond that had been forged.

Jazintu could communicate with the baby dragon from a distance. She could tell Emeraldesa knew that she was on her way and she could 'hear' the dragon's response. Eeeps, coos and clucking squeaking sounds came to her. Even though she was over 700 metres away the excited anticipation of the dragon was clear and unmistakable.

Emeraldesa ate well and was nourished by the food, her body rapidly developing. The young dragon had nearly doubled in size. With her wings becoming bigger, the dragon hugged Jazintu gently by folding its wings around her, taking in the food and releasing her once each meal was finished. The trust between each other was complete.

Then one day after the wings unfolded they were held down gently, as if in an offering. Jazintu wondered, "Is she inviting me to climb on, will she teach me to fly?"

As she stood before the dragon with its wings held down, Jazintu felt a mixture of excitement and uncertainty. She had nurtured the dragon since it had moved to the barn, and their connection was now one of complete mutual trust. Faced with the opportunity to ride and fly on its back, she realized the magnitude of the moment.

Taking a deep breath, she approached Emeraldesa cautiously, filled with both excitement and apprehension. She had observed the dragon's movements closely over the months and understood her behaviour to a certain extent. However, mounting and flying on her own dragon was an entirely new experience - one that required communication and skill. She had only been a pigeon passenger a couple of times on her brothers' rides. Doing her own solo with a young dragon was a much bigger deal.

She had begun to understand the dragon's rhythm and started mimicking its motions on the ground. She would extend her arms like wings, tilting and shifting her body to mirror the dragon's potential flight. Jazintu's movements enticed and invited the dragon to fly. It was a process of developing a deep kinaesthetic connection, attuning herself to the dragon's energy and essence and Emeraldesa to hers.

During their daily interactions, the dragon reciprocated her efforts. It patiently guided her, demonstrating the subtle adjustments of its wings, the way it positioned its body for take-off and landing. Through these gentle gestures, the dragon communicated its wisdom, teaching Jazintu the art of flight without words.

As days turned into weeks and weeks into months, their relationship grew stronger. With each passing day, she felt closer and closer to the dragon, as if their souls were intertwined.

She learned to mount the dragon with confidence, finding the perfect spot between its powerful wings, where she could feel the warmth of its body and the rhythmic beat of its heart.

She knew to position herself right behind the dragon's folded wings. Sensing her intention, the dragon shifted slightly, giving her more space and lowering one wing to give her a way to lever herself up. She would pull herself onto the wing, and then up onto its back, then ease herself into position. Emeraldesa's muscles flexed beneath her and they would be ready to take flight.

Jazintu reached out and stroked the dragon's sleek scales, conveying her affection. They shared a telepathic connection, an unspoken understanding between human and dragon. Using this method she imagined them both outside the barn. It had worked and they were both outside.

With a gentle command, "Up," she urged the dragon to take off. The dragon sensed her excitement as if in answer, cooed, acknowledging the request.
The dragon spread its wings wide, ready to take flight. With a surge of adrenaline and a leap of faith, they soared into the sky together. The cold air bit her face and she was exhilarated.

The powerful wings beat against the air, lifting them higher and higher. The girl clung onto the dragon's back, feeling a mix of exhilaration and awe.
As they flew straight up from outside the barn, it became a small dot, its roof fading as they went higher and higher.

The wind rushed past them, and she marvelled at the breathtaking view. As they soared through the clouds, the dragon guided her, adjusting its movements to help her find her balance. It was a symbiotic relationship, a dance of trust and cooperation.

Confident now, with her body snug against the dragon, Jazintu leaned forward, lifting her head slightly to let her hair blow back. She felt a sense of freedom and was exhilarated.

As they returned, descending to the yard, Jazintu hugged tightly, not wanting to slip off as the dragon's nose pointed downward. With a plop they were grounded, the dust rising around them from the sheer weight of Emeraldesa.

Once having alighted, Jazintu stood beside her and patted her head gently. The dragon responded by nuzzling her hand, its eyes reflecting warmth and understanding. She let out a small contented blaze of fire.

A new ritual was carried out daily now; after feeding her dragon, they did a short flight, returning to the cliff and landing on the rocky outcrop over the cave. No other dragons were seen, but Jazintu wondered if the young dragon was going there to look for its mother.

With each flight, Jazintu grew more confident, her initial apprehension giving way to a profound sense of freedom and a growing intimate connection with Emeraldesa.
Confident in their flight and body connection the two enjoyed their time together as they flew regularly. Jazintu, encouraged by her confidence and faultless flights and landings, felt ready to fly further now. She wondered if Emeraldesa was up for it too.
Early one morning Jazintu packed extra food supplies and a flask. She shouldered her bag and with a sense of adventure approached the barn. Emeraldesa was already outside stretching her wings, her scales gently glimmering, reflecting the light of the Sun.

As Jazintu settled into a comfortable position on the dragon's back, she looked down at the majestic wings, now fully extended.

Each time they took off she marvelled at how they could soar through the skies. She knew she had to trust in the dragon absolutely. Jazintu had to completely surrender to the dragon's control.

As Jazintu and the Emeraldesa soared through the sky, Jazintu was in awe of the sight below her. The cliffs stretched out in a rugged expanse, their jagged edges cutting into the foamy waves below. She was so high up and the wide dragon's wings carried them effortlessly through the air.

Jazintu couldn't help but feel a sense of wonder as they swept along the coastline. She could see the world from a perspective few ever had the privilege to witness. The vast expanse of the ocean sparkled under the sunlight, its colours ranging from deep blues to shimmering greens. As they glided along the coastline, the sound of the waves crashing against the cliffs and the distant cries of seabirds added to the symphony of nature that surrounded them.

Jazintu could feel the warmth of the creature beneath her, a reassuring reminder that she was not alone on this incredible journey. The dragon's scales glowed green with hints of silver and gold, its powerful muscles flexing beneath Jazintu.

Emeraldesa was a wonderful ride. Jazintu's body fitted snugly on her dragon, the soft hide of the dragon comfortable, held secure by a gentle pressure of her knees. The glistening leathery skin caught light in the Sun. The dragon's spikes were a handy grip hold as they wove up and down. The width of the dragon's wings was immense despite the young age of her companion. Their emerald green and aqua tints shimmered and shone as the pair rose and dived, enjoying their ride.

Jazintu couldn't have asked for a more magnificent dragon or a more unforgettable adventure.

Reticent to return too early, the two landed at a quiet cove. Jazintu lay on the golden sand next to her dragon, both grazing on the picnic of cold meats and honeyed goat's milk. They dozed afterwards, the Sun's warmth cloaking them like a comfortable blanket.

As the daylight reached its summit and the Sun was overhead they made their way home. Landing in private behind the barn, Jazintu dismounted.

Feeling elated and still tingling with the excitement of the flight, Jazintu changed her clothes to the clean set she had hidden in the barn. She had timed her return to the homestead well. She was in time for the evening meal with her family and was glad that the private location of the now disused barn allowed her secrecy of her activities.
The distance of the barn combined with it being hidden by a tall row of thick trees meant no-one bothered to venture there anymore.

With each flight, Jazintu grew more connected and she felt a profound sense of love for her dragon friend. In time, Jazintu and her dragon became inseparable. The bond they shared was not only one of trust but also of mutual growth and friendship.

And so, the girl and her dragon continued their journeys, their spirits intertwined, as they traversed the skies.

They were travelling further and further each trip.

The ease of their time together and their flights gave Jazintu a wonderful sense of freedom and excitement.

She never tired of the joy and wonder she felt as they glided through the air. She loved the feeling of weightlessness. She felt she had become one with the dragon and she knew their destinies were linked.

With every flight, she grew more skilled, navigating the air currents and understanding the dragon's silent cues.

Emeraldesa became her guide, her protector, and her confidante.

All the while Jazintu kept her dragon secret from her brothers Jasper and Mordan, who had their own dragons on the other side of the homestead. She hadn't breathed a word to Lazura either. She knew she would have to tell them at some point, but for now she was simply enjoying their special time alone together.

She was glad that she hadn't told anyone about her dragon yet. Somehow, it being a secret added to her feelings of exhilaration.

Unbeknown to Jazintu, there were some who knew of the young dragon's existence. Mordan and Jasper's dragons had sensed and smelt the new arrival. After a flight with their riders, when they were on their own and the brothers had retired indoors, they had investigated. The two huge creatures had swooped down to the barn, sniffed around it and peered through the crack of the barn doors. They saw Emeraldesa sleeping deeply after her own flight, unaware of their presence. Seeing how young the dragon was they had retreated, instinctively knowing that its small size was no threat to them.

Chapter 4

The brothers flew with their dragons weekly, on their one day off from the farm chores. Sunday, late in the afternoon, they would take their swords and simulate battles on the ground with their dragons standing guard by their sides.

Jasper and Mordan regularly enjoyed their sparring sessions with each other. It was a good day for a flight and they decided to 'warm up' by having a short sword fight. The Sun's warm rays glinted off their swords as their blades clashed and echoed with each strike.
Their movements were fluid and practiced, the result of many years of training together.
Mordan's style was calculated and precise. His strikes were aimed to exploit any weaknesses in his brother's defence.

The younger brother Jasper, on the other hand, fought with a more impulsive and energetic approach, relying on his agility to evade attacks and counter with swift moves.

As the sparring continued, their laughter mixed with the sound of steel on steel. They were not fighting to harm each other, rather to challenge and improve their skills. Knowing each other well, they communicated without words, anticipating each other's moves and adapting their strategies in real time.

After a particularly frenetic exchange, they paused to catch their breath, sweat glistening on their brows. Mordan grinned, his chest heaving. "You're getting better, little brother," he said between breaths.
Jasper chuckled, wiping his forehead with his sleeve. "And you're not getting any slower, big brother."

Their banter was interrupted by the sound of approaching footsteps. Their sister, Jazintu, had been watching them spar. She approached with a proud smile, "I see you two are at it again," she remarked.

The brothers exchanged glances before sheathing their swords. Mordan spoke, his voice filled with playful annoyance, "You know, if you had joined us, we could have made it a fair fight."

Jazintu rolled her eyes. "Oh please, I've seen enough of your 'fair fights' to know better". She then turned to Jasper. "But I must say, your form is improving. Maybe one day you'll win!"

Jasper grinned, clearly pleased by the compliment. "Just you wait, sister. I'll beat him soon enough."

Their shared love for the art of combat and their unbreakable connection as family made every training session a way to hone their skills safely.

"What have you been up to this fine day Jazintu?" Mordan asked.

"Oh, I have been out exploring the coastline," she replied. "I trust you will enjoy your flights."

Jasper and Mordan approached their dragons. Their swords fitted snugly on the dragon's saddles.

Ready for their ride now, they alighted and made clicking sounds for their dragons to rise. The sound of huge flapping wings and delighted cries carried them into the sky.

Their swords were a testament to the blacksmith's skill, crafted from the finest steel and honed to perfection. The blades held a deadly edge, ready to cleave through armour and flesh alike. Yet, these swords weren't just tools of warfare; they were also a symbol of honour and heritage, passed down through generations.

They had sheathed their swords in intricately designed scabbards. These scabbards were more than simple holders; they were tailored to fit snugly against their bodies, allowing them to move freely while keeping the swords secure and ready for action. The design was adaptable to fit neatly and securely on the saddle of each dragon. The sheathed sword fitted into a slot that kept it secure but able to move as they flew.

The dragons' saddles were made with the same craftsmanship. Designed not only for comfort during flight but also for practicality.

Each saddle had specially crafted slots and loops where the brothers could secure additional equipment and weapons such as daggers. The mounts were a seamless blend of function and aesthetics, with rich leather and decorative metallic accents complementing the dragons' scales.

The brothers spoke to their dragons in a series of distinct clicks and whistles. These were no ordinary sounds; they were a unique language the dragons understood, a language that conveyed commands and camaraderie. The dragons, massive and powerful, responded to their riders' signals with a rumble of approval.

Jazintu had watched as the boys and their dragons made a special lift-off. They used a technique that made the dragons super responsive. With a synchronized rhythm, Mordan and Jasper drew their swords partially from their scabbards, allowing the blades to catch the sunlight. The act of drawing their swords and creating the distinct clicking sound wasn't just a command for the dragons; it was a tradition, a ritual that signalled their readiness to take flight and face whatever challenges awaited them.

The dragons spread their wings and rose into the sky, the brothers still holding their swords at an angle. Then once they were level and flying smoothing, they sheathed them in place again, their hands steady despite the rush of wind. The clicking sound echoed in the air, a harmonious melody that resonated with the beating of dragon wings.

Jazintu smiled to herself, with the happy knowledge of her own dragon tucked up safely in the barn. A mound of old straw shielded any view from prying eyes. She had also taken the extra precaution of bolting and locking the doors so that no curious eyes could spy what lay within. She didn't want to take any chances of someone stumbling across Emeraldesa.

Chapter 5

The brothers had flown along the coastline and would later fly inland. In the west a terrible scene was unfolding. Other dragons were in the air, but this time they were wild ones, fighter dragons that were not bonded to humans. A large number of them were in full flight.

The brothers had taken a well-known route to fly. The coast was scenic and the rolling hills of the inland were a delight to cross over. Mordan and Jasper had met up with some other dragons and riders. As they had flown inland their kinfolk from neighbouring parishes joined to make up a small group.
The riders and dragons flew in formation as they approached a village under attack.

On the ground were many inhabitants amidst a simple layout of huts, yards and pens. People were scattering.
Once the villagers had seen the fire-breathing fighter dragons in the distance they knew it was a matter of

minutes before their homes were burnt and scorched to the ground.

They knew they had to flee for their lives, abandoning their homes and possessions in order to survive. The threat was imminent, there was no time to waste.

Closer now the ominous shapes took form against the horizon. Fighter dragons, fearsome and powerful, soared through the sky with an air of undeniable menace.

The Belonghi's hearts sank; their village was about to become a battleground. It was catastrophic. They were about to be caught in the crossfire of the fire-fighter dragons, a force of nature that was far beyond their control.

Many of the families had heard tales of the destructive capabilities of these dragons, stories passed down through generations. They knew that the breath of these mighty creatures could unleash flames that would reduce their homes to ashes. It was a terror that had haunted them as nightmares, and now it was becoming a chilling reality.

As the fighter dragons drew nearer, the villagers could almost feel the heat of their fiery breath. The air seemed hotter. Time seemed to slow down as they watched the dragons approach, their massive wings casting vast shadows on the land below.

Panic and despair rippled through the people as they grabbed the hands of their loved ones and children and ran.

There was no heroic stand, no last-minute defence that they could muster. The villagers were unprepared to face such a formidable threat. Their only option was to retreat, to find safety in distance and hope their lives would be spared from the dragon's wrath.

As they fled, some cast backward glances, their eyes filled with a mixture of fear and disbelief at the disaster that was unfolding. Their once-thriving community was being reduced to a barren landscape.

The small huts and the community hall furled and snapped in flames, the air was thick with dark smoke and animals ran in all directions. The fighter dragons left nothing untouched. Very quickly the village was transformed to a place of charred ruins.

Chickens, dogs and goats released from their pens ran hither and thither, unsure of what direction to take. Unused to their newfound freedom but taking flight for survival they made their escape.

The fighter dragons had begun killing only recently. In the past dragons and people had lived on the planet peacefully. It was a mystery as to why they were now attacking villages and killing again without mercy.

It had not been heard of in recent times, only in tales handed down from past generations.

Many discussions had failed to find any reason for the dragons' behaviour and the incidents had been growing as the number of the dragons increased.

To the east another set of dragons approached. This time it was dragons with riders approaching.

The community gathered on the edges of their smouldering village stunned and speechless.

The fighter dragons had retreated, having little left to aim at, the village now mostly in ruins.

Children were crying and mothers consoled them, grateful to have saved their lives.

Mordan and Jasper had seen the rising and drifting smoke from the village not far from where they were flying. They leant sideways and pressed their knees into the dragons, who responded by changing direction and flying westwards.

Certain that the dragons had now left the area, the villagers dragged items out of smouldering ruins and began gathering in the centre. As the friendly dragons approached, panic gave way to a sense of relief as they observed the stark difference. These dragons bore riders on their backs, their figures distinct against the sky. The villagers watched with curiosity and hope as the dragons with riders drew nearer. Help was at hand.

The news of the second group of dragons had spread quickly, and the traumatised community were ready to meet their neighbours. They huddled in the centre of what was once their bustling village. Stunned and speechless, they stood amidst the devastation, their faces etched with a complex blend of emotions. The children, frightened by the chaos and destruction, continued to cry in the arms of their mothers, who offered comfort in the midst of the turmoil.

The small group of dragons circled downwards, Mordan and Jasper in the lead. The dragon landing was welcome, in distinct contrast to the fear they felt at the fire and destruction they had just experienced. Only a small child whimpered fearing another attack.

Mordan's dragon landed gently, and he stepped down, waiting for permission to approach the villagers. Jasper also alighted. They stood silently, taking stock of the destruction surrounding them.

Mordan was signalled with permission to approach and he communicated to the others to also land.

As the remaining dragons descended, their massive wings caused dark shadows over the bleak desolation. The villagers held their breath. The landing was achieved with perfect grace. In one accord, the remainder of the small group landed simultaneously.

Slow purposeful steps brought the riders closer to the gathered crowd, their presence radiating a sense of calm and reassurance. The villagers knew that these visitors were not there to bring further harm, but rather to offer support and aid. The tension in the air gradually eased as the riders were recognised. Their neighbours approached conveying messages of friendship.

With the riders standing before them, the villagers found their voices. Questions and murmurs filled the air as they sought to understand the purpose of the unexpected arrival. The expressions on the faces of all the riders were sympathetic, and their words carried the soothing tone of understanding. They explained how they had spied the smoke and understood the villagers' plight. Mordan and Jasper offered condolences but also practical help. "We are here for you, neighbours. Anything we can do, we will help. You can shelter with us for a while and rebuild."

As the communication unfolded, a sense of relief washed over the community. They had support, were not alone in this destructive struggle, their closest neighbours had come to their aid. Their island neighbours had extended a helping hand during their darkest hour. The fire had been so intense there was little left, with only a few timber walls still smouldering. With virtually nothing left, they would need all the help they could get.

The villagers were slowly coming to terms with the scale of the disaster. The children's tears began to subside. And as the Sun dipped below the horizon, tensions eased. They had help, the knights from Ridgecliff were there for them.
Amidst the remnants of the devastated hamlet, the village elder, a wise woman named Elvsbreath, sat with

her back against the stone well that had somehow managed to withstand the destruction. Around her, families and individuals came together to commiserate with each other. They began sharing the losses they had all suffered. Telling the tales of how they closely escaped death.

As the people gathered, their faces were etched with sorrow and disbelief. The two brothers commanded attention loudly declaring refuge on behalf of their own family. Mordan and Jasper, with their walk synchronized, approached the wise woman. With a shared understanding that transcended words, they spoke almost simultaneously, their voices carrying a resolute resolve. "Let us help you."

"We offer all from your village refuge at ours," Mordan began. "We can provide campsites in the outbuildings and around the homestead for as long as you need, or until you rebuild the village of Eastabahn," Jasper continued.

His gaze locked onto the wise woman's eyes. Their words were a pledge, a commitment born out of compassion and a deep sense of community.

Elvsbreath, the village elder, listened carefully to their proposition. Her eyes, weathered and wise, held a spark of gratitude as she gazed at the brothers. She nodded slowly, her lips curving into a small, appreciative smile. "Your kindness and generosity in the face of adversity warms my heart," Elvsbreath spoke with calm authority. "To open your home and offer shelter to all of us who have lost so much is true evidence of the strength of our bonds as a community across the island."

Everyone's expressions were slowly shifting from sorrow to a glimmer of hope. The brothers' offer held the promise of a new beginning, a chance to rebuild with the support of their neighbouring villagers.

Elvsbreath extended her hand, her palm open in a gesture of unity. "We accept your offer, with much gratitude. You have brought us hope," she said. "May our combined strength and resilience see us through this challenging time and may the bonds we forge in adversity be unbreakable."

With a solemn nod, the brothers clasped Elvsbreath's hand in agreement, sealing the pact of solidarity. As the Sun slowly dipped below the horizon, it cast a warm glow over the village that had once stood and would rise again.

The villagers were still in shock, but began to move with some renewed purpose, fuelled by the collective determination to rebuild, to support one another, and to find solace and strength.

Dragons had landed well-spaced around, a procession of people made their way to their rides. They climbed on knowing at least they would have shelter for the night. But they remained uncertain of what the future would hold.

The dragons, towering and magnificent, waited patiently as the villagers mounted, providing a sense of security and comfort amidst the chaos.

The villagers held no fear of these dragons who presented so differently from the others. Their bodily expression was inviting, with lowered heads and gently, partly closed eyes. Their elaborate saddles were a sign of their domesticity and a reminder of their status of being ridden.

As the villagers settled onto the dragon saddles, the creatures stretched their wings, readying for flight. The anticipation was palpable, a mixture of excitement and nervousness that coursed through the air. With powerful beats of their wings, the dragons lifted off the ground, ascending into the sky with a grace that defied their massive size.

Chapter 6

The journey was slow and deliberate, each dragon mindful of its precious additional cargo. Each dragon carried two or three people and numerous bags of belongings. The flight back to the homestead was a journey of sad reflection for the villagers as they abandoned what was once their home. Some gave a final glance at the ruins.

As they flew high above their land and the remaining outbuildings, it all grew smaller and smaller. The dragons, led by Jasper and Mordan, made their way slowly home.

Landing at Ridgecliff in a circle the villagers were able to gather once more, this time in their new environment.

With their hearts heavy from loss and their minds racing with questions about the future, the villagers dismounted from the dragons. The promise of shelter brought momentary relief, but the unknown that lay ahead was a weight they could not easily shake.

Arriving at their destination, the dragons encircled the villagers once more. This time, however, they stood in solidarity, with the promise of refuge and a fresh start. The numerous outbuildings close to the homestead, now illuminated by soft torchlight, radiated a sense of warmth and welcome.

Once descended from the dragons' backs, they cast curious glances around their new surroundings. Uncertainty still lingered, but it was tempered by the knowledge that they were not alone in this journey.
Their neighbours and their dragons had become guardians and allies. The villagers had a chance to rebuild, to forge a new community under the watchful eyes of these majestic, powerful creatures.

Gathering in the circle formed by the dragons, the villagers looked at each other with a renewed sense of determination. The future was uncertain, but they were united by their shared experiences and their collective will to persevere. The dragons stood as a reminder that even in the face of adversity, there was strength in unity, and hope in unexpected allies.

The dragons were of various colours. Deep magenta with silvery scales, dark blue with shiny black tips on their wings, tan with golden hues and matching golden eyes. Their breath was warm, blowing a soft breeze over the campers. They leant their heads on their sides, resting.

In the glow of the torchlight and under the protective presence of the dragons, Jasper and Mordan worked together to build a large central fire for the villagers. As the fire crackled to life, the flames danced and cast a comforting warmth that contrasted with the cool night air.

Around the fire, makeshift seating was arranged, fashioned from logs and sturdy wooden crates.

The villagers, wearied by their recent ordeals, found solace in the flickering light and the promise of a good meal. The dragons, their forms silhouetted against the darkness, added an element of safeguarding and reassurance.

Jasper and Mordan, their faces illuminated by the firelight, worked together with a sense of purpose. The brothers were no strangers to hardship, having endured their own trials, and now they were determined to make their fellow villagers as welcome as they could.

Jazintu was also busy making the newcomers comfortable. She gathered bedding in the form of rugs and cloth. Beds were made up in the outbuildings and under the verandah of the homestead. Children ran around her and jumped on the bedding, trying it out.

Large cast iron pots were placed over a fire, and the aroma of stew soon began to fill the air. The scent was comforting and enticing. The pots were filled with hearty ingredients, carefully selected to provide energy and nourishment. The children followed Jazintu back to the central gathering.

As the beef stew simmered, the villagers gathered around the fire, their faces reflecting a mixture of weariness and gratitude. The sight of a familiar setting and the camaraderie of a shared fire helped ease the tension. Neighbours exchanged glances and spoke with encouragement, determined to make the best of things. They put on brave faces and spoke with confidence as much to convince themselves as for their family around them.

Jazintu and Lazura, mindful of the villagers' needs, had ladled the stew into bowls, feeding the children first. As food was passed around and villagers had settled in to savour the hearty meal, a sense of unity permeated the air. The warmth of the food mirrored the warmth of the fire and the newfound bonds forming among the villagers and their neighbours. Conversations flowed, people began to visibly relax and occasional laughs carried across the campsites. The dragons, ever watchful with just one eye closed, surrounded the villagers as silent sentinels.

Under the stars and by the light of the fire, the villagers found comfort. The support and the hot stew warmed both bodies and spirits, rekindling the flames of resilience that would guide them through the challenges ahead. After the meal Lazura prepared herbal teas and poured cordial for the children.

In this moment, surrounded by friends old and new, they found strength in each other and in the promise of a shared journey toward rebuilding their lives. The sense of camaraderie was comforting. And having been given cloaks and rugs many made makeshift beds around the fire and laid down to rest.

In the roomy homestead, the resident family gathered - Jasper, Mordan, their sisters, Jazintu and Lazura - along with the village elders and a few others. The events that had unfolded were recounted. Around them, the strong stone walls which had borne witness to many past years of shared memories, were now the backdrop to the troubling issues that loomed over them all.

Death by dragon fire, flash destruction to ash. The tales were morbid and did not last long, it was too distressing.

Words of sympathy were offered and hugs were exchanged in an attempt to ease the burden.

Lazura and Jazintu sat together next to some other young female cousins. Lazura brushed the hair of a young girl in order to provide comfort and a sense of normality. She had always liked it when her parents had been alive, the soothing effect of a brush and the gentle touch of a hand on her head.
The closest cousins from the nearby village had been given beds to share in the homestead, a place of security and comfort after their ordeal.

The fighter fire-wreaking dragons, once considered mythical creatures, had become a very real threat. In the past, fear had only arisen from the horrific tales being told. Many had thought them only a fable to scare children from venturing too far and to liven up evenings of storytelling. But fighter dragons that had razed villages were now a real and present danger.
The sombre mood of Jazintu's family mirrored the gravity of the situation. They waited until the youngest

was finally asleep. Then their conversations circled around the same pivotal question: how could they protect their own village from the marauding dragons? The situation was dire, the danger was closer than it had ever been. It was a challenging situation that required unity, strategy, and perhaps unconventional solutions.

As ideas were shared, their voices held a mix of urgency and determination.

"We cannot simply wait for the next attack," Jasper spoke, his voice firm. "We must find a way to defend ourselves, to shield our homes and families from the destruction these dragons bring."

Mordan nodded in agreement, his brow furrowed in thought. "But how do we combat creatures that can wield fire with such devastating power," he questioned? His eyes searching others faces for answers.

Their sister, Lazura, whose wisdom and insights were highly regarded by the family, spoke up. "We need to gather information about these dragons, their patterns, their vulnerabilities. Knowledge is our greatest weapon, and it will guide us in formulating a plan."

Jazintu was an eager listener to the conversations. She felt that she and her dragon were going to play an integral part in the future that was unfolding for their neighbours.

Somehow, the young dragon she had bonded with was bound to be a part of what was to come. She just knew it in her bones. She just wasn't sure how their part would play out yet. Time would tell.

In the early morning, when the light was barely apparent, a gathering formed naturally. The elders of Ridgecliff along with those from neighbouring Eastabahn sat around the rekindled fire. The village elders, wise figures with years of experience, listened to each other intently. Their expressions revealed a mix of concern and hope.

"We've faced challenges before," one elder, Barahan, began. "We've overcome trouble through unity and resourcefulness. We must remember that." They agreed and a consensus formed based on seeking more information to better arm them.

They discussed ways to divert the dragons' attention, potential ways to weaken or deter them, and strategies to collaborate with additional neighbouring villages in order to strengthen their defences.

Ideas flowed, and plans began to take shape. The atmosphere shifted from uncertainty to one of purpose. All were bound by their community commitment and were determined to face this threat head-on and find a way to ensure the safety of all.

The discussions continued, fuelled by the shared belief that together they could rise above the challenge. The fire in their hearts matched the one in burning in their midst, demonstrating their resilience and their unbreakable resolve to protect what was theirs.

Plans to return to their charred village and find anything of use was discussed. But the main focus was on how to protect everyone in Ridgecliff.

They agreed that in the coming days, their plans would evolve, strategies would be refined, and preparations would be made. The journey ahead would be daunting, but they faced it with the strength of a united family and united villages, ready to strategise and deter the dragon fire that threatened to consume their homes and their way of life.

The plan was clear. Dragons and riders would seek and find out the behaviour of the fighter dragons, and come back, train their own and be a stronger resistance to any future attack.

Chapter 7

With a plan taking shape, a select few emerged from the discussions, chosen to undertake a crucial journey. Barahan led a group, gathering his fittest villagers to join the band formed by Mordan and Jordan. The task was to venture out beyond their familiar territories, seeking out neighbouring villages that had faced similar dragon attacks. Their mission: to gather information, learn from their experiences, and identify any potential vulnerabilities or patterns that could be exploited to protect their own village.

The group chosen for this mission consisted of fit and skilled individuals, each contributing their unique strengths to the endeavour. Among them were experienced trackers, keen observers, resourceful thinkers, and renowned sword fighters. As they gathered their provisions and prepared to set out, both apprehension and excitement filled the air.

The journey would take them through unfamiliar landscapes, to villages that were remote and distant. Each step would be a chance to learn, to listen to the stories of those who had faced the fire-breathing dragons firsthand. The information they sought was crucial: insights into the dragons' behaviour, their vulnerabilities, and any strategies that had been effective in fending them off.

As the large group set out, their hearts were heavy with responsibility yet buoyed by a shared sense of purpose. The road stretched before them, winding through forests, over hills, and across rivers. Their path led them to villages that would hopefully have information to share, tales of survival and strategies born out of necessity. Ways and means they hoped to learn in order to strengthen their cause.

They travelled widely and over several weeks.
They listened as villagers recounted their encounters with the dragons. Some spoke of rare sightings and near misses, while others shared more harrowing

stories of destruction and loss. From these firsthand accounts, patterns began to emerge. There were times of day when the dragons were more active, behaviours that seemed to trigger their attacks, and potential weaknesses that could be exploited.

With each village they visited, the group's knowledge grew. They gathered important information on the dragons' patterns, compiled insights, and engaged in discussions that spanned many late nights by firesides. The stories were sobering, a reminder of the threat that lurked on the fringes of their lives.

Their trip had taken them on nearly a full circumference of the island. It wasn't far now to fly back to Ridgecliff. The salt freshened the air as they neared the ocean, and the dragons lifted their wings higher in anticipation of reaching home. Their speed quickened as they neared their beloved cliffs and the plateau that formed a long ridge above the sea.

As they returned to the village, the group carried with them a wealth of information and a renewed sense of purpose. The gathered knowledge was a treasure trove of potential solutions. Back in their own community, they would share what they had learned, analysing the data and strategizing on how to implement new defences and tactics.

Warm greetings were made, hugs and laughter rang out during feasting over several days. The riders rested and recouped. Then it was time.
Group leaders gathered and over many nights shared their valuable insights and began to formulate a defence plan. A clever plan emerged. It would involve specialist training for dragon and rider teams.

As the villagers shared what they had learned about the fighter dragons' they perfected their strategies. The dragons' fire, once considered only a force of devastation, was soon to diminish in its potent threat.

Knowledge was power. How fire was applied to the dragon fights was now a weapon to be wielded with precision and control. The group now had specialised defence approaches to utilize when engaging in dragon war. The air was thick with a sense of anticipation, but also determination. This was a fight they could not afford to lose. Thanks to the special master plan there was now a much greater chance to win without loss of life.

The villagers worked tirelessly, constructing defence mechanisms and fortifying vulnerable areas. Barahan assisted in coordinating with the larger dragons, developing communication signals and plans to ensure a synchronized attack.
Being of large stature and well respected in his village, others trusted him. He was a strong leader and there was no hesitation from others to follow his directions.

Baharan, Jasper and Mordan worked late into every evening, honing and finalising the attack approaches.

And so, as the time came for the final stage of their plan, the villagers and their dragon allies stood ready. The larger dragons, with their size, strength, and controlled fire, made a considerable force. The villagers themselves were armed with fierce determination.

After several weeks everyone was finally ready. A final meal was shared and, as the Sun set, the chosen dragons spread their wings. The time had come to face the fire-breathing dragons that had destroyed their homes. The atmosphere was tense with the weight of their purpose, but also the belief in their collective strength.

With the biggest dragons leading the charge, the villagers embarked on the confrontation they had prepared so tirelessly for. The battle that was about to unfold would be a test of their planning in order to protect what was theirs.
The villagers and their dragon allies had practised by flying and fighting with their swords, side by side. They were now a force to be reckoned with.

They were determined to secure their future against the fire-breathing threat that had destroyed their lives.

The plan was clever and calculated. It revolved around utilising a select group of dragons with the larger and more mature individuals to confront the fire-breathing fighter dragons. This group of dragons possessed not only size and strength but also a formidable fire-emitting force themselves. It could be harnessed in their defence when needed.

The fiery breath of their select group of dragons indeed held the potential to counterattack the dangerous fire-breathing fighter dragons effectively. The research they had gathered was instrumental in identifying the vulnerabilities of these fighter dragons, which included six key factors.

There was limited fire resistance in the enemy fighter dragons.

While the fighter fire-breathing dragons were known for their ability to spew flames, they were not immune to fire themselves. The intense heat of fire breath could be a vulnerability when unleashed against them.

Size and speed were next. The enemy dragons, though formidable, tended to be much larger and bulkier due to their fiery capabilities.
This size disadvantage could make them slower and less agile in combat, making them susceptible to attacks from more agile opponents.

Fire-breath cooldown was an opportunity. Observations had revealed that the larger fire-breathing dragons had a cooldown period after using their fire-breath attack on each occasion. During this cooldown, they would be temporarily unable to unleash another fiery assault for several minutes, leaving them vulnerable to counterattacks.

Energy drain was another factor. Spewing fire required a significant amount of energy, and the fighter dragons could be exploited in this weakness. By engaging in prolonged combat and forcing the fire-breathing dragons to continuously use their breath attacks, their adversaries could become exhausted. They could even be depleted of fire.

Close combat vulnerability was in the Belonghi people's favour. The fighter fire-breathing dragons might have been more proficient at long-ranged fire attacks. Engaging them in close combat, where their fiery breath was less effective, could be a viable strategy. The younger and somewhat smaller fire-breathing dragons tended to engage in close combat as their flames simply didn't travel as far. So those were dragons that could be attacked first. And the midsized villagers' dragons would beat them easily.

The final area of weakness was the type of villages the dragons chose. The research showed that fire-breathing dragons had preferences of poorer places with less defences. They were communities that were made up of many wooden huts with some small yards. Largely undefended due to having no stone or other fortress for protection.

By being aware of these preferences, the fighters could exploit weaknesses in their approaches. The new dragon force would fly first to these poorer villages,
located in the lower lands. In that way they could more quickly intercept the killer dragons. They would know where they were likely to attack and be ready to defend.

Armed with all this knowledge, the select group of dragons, under the expert guidance of the villagers, were well-prepared to counterattack the dangerous fighter dragons and defend villages effectively.

The criteria for selecting the dragons for the knight-riders were specific: they had to be fully mature, at least five years old, and equipped with the ability to wield their own fire-breathing power. These dragons were not only physically imposing, with a grandeur that set them apart, but they were also equipped with the tools necessary for this high-stakes confrontation.

The chosen battle dragons were indeed a sight to behold. Their wingspans created broad shadows as they took to the sky. The scales that adorned their bodies were thicker and shinier, a sign of their age and resilience. These dragons had weathered the passage of time, growing stronger and wiser with each passing year.

They were a breed that was smaller and more agile than the enemy fighter dragons but still formidable and fierce.

Their eyes held a deep golden hue, reflecting the wisdom and determination that came with their mature age. These were creatures that had seen countless mock battles, making them tough and resilient. Their gaze held a sense of purpose that matched that of the villagers who stood alongside them.

The plan hinged on choosing the right times to engage the other dragons in combat. Timing was crucial, as was the element of surprise. The mature midsize dragons would need to rely on their own strength and fire-emitting power to subdue the attackers, preventing further destruction and harm to the remaining villages.

All the riders, including the villagers and knights, had trained together on dragons, forging a bond that transcended species. They had practiced flight formations, honed their communication techniques and perfected their strategies for engaging the enemy dragons. The dragons' fire, once a force of devastation, was now a weapon to be wielded with precision and control.

The villagers had worked tirelessly and fortified vulnerable areas in their plan. All was well coordinated between dragons and riders, ensuring a synchronized attack. The air was thick with determination.
Everything depended on them working together and their rehearsed approaches working effectively.
With the dragons leading the charge the battle could be won. When the time came to fight amidst fire and fury, the villagers and their dragon protectors would fight side by side. They were now a force to be reckoned with.

Confident in securing their future against the fire-breathing threat that had all but ruined their lives.

Chapter 8

There were five mature dragons as leaders, and these were magnificent to behold. Each of the dragons had a different colour and their individual beauty and detail were identifiable from a light that shone from inside. The thick shiny scales had an opaque glow. Their eyes were deep and golden. And when they were in fight mode the glow inside each intensified, radiating throughout their whole body, all the way to their wingtips. A test roar of flames emitted in unison. Fire streamed from them with a crackling that lighted their whole torso.

The dragons represented majestic symbols of strength and power. The light that shone from inside cast an ethereal glow, illuminating the air around them. The refracted light created an aura of otherworldly elegance.

Their eyes, deep and golden glowed with power and portent. They were windows into the souls of these creatures, and as the dragons prepared for the confrontation, the eyes glowed brighter.

In unison the dragon force took off, flying high and fast towards a village they hoped was yet untouched by the enemy's deadly charring blows. The village was a tiny one on the low plains of Belonghi. A group of twenty huts were clustered around a central open community space. The dragons and riders had arrived just in time. The fire-breathing killer dragons were approaching from the south.

When the time came to engage in battle, the transformation was awe-inspiring.
The internal glow within each dragon increased, creating an intense luminescence that radiated through their entire bodies. From the tips of their wings to the ends of their tails, the dragons were bathed in a radiant light. It was a sight that evoked both reverence and a profound understanding of the incredible power they wielded.

As the dragons entered fight mode, fire erupted from them with a force that defied imagination. The flames formed in arcs of brilliant light, crackling and roaring as they consumed the air around them. An inferno speared forth and at the same time illuminated the body of the dragons. One by one they circled and prepared to directly aim at the fighter dragons.

Their flight was synchronized, evidence of their training with their riders and the villagers. With a swift and calculated precision, they dived, their fiery power focused and concentrated. The flames shot out in blazes of brilliance, aiming with accuracy at the destructive fire-breathing dragons.

The thunder of dragons took the fighter dragons by surprise.
The battle that ensued was a whirlwind of searing heat and movement. The dragons on the side of the villagers roared with fury, their flames meeting those of their adversaries. The clash of fire and the resounding roars

echoed through the air, a symphony of light and screeching.

Amidst the chaos, the villagers below watched with bated breath, their hearts pounding in fear with the beat of the battle. Dragons, once only symbols of fear, were now also champions of their cause, unleashing their fiery might.
As the flames danced and the battle raged on, all of the dragons' brilliance lit up their entire forms. The sky was painted with bursts of orange, blue and red fire, a dazzling display.

With every dive and every burst of flame, the dragon saviours drew closer to victory. Their efforts demonstrated their power and courage. Their single intent was to protect to the death. The battle was long and intense, but the defenders' tactics were working, the enemy fire-breathing fighter dragons showed signs of weakness.

As the battle reached its crescendo, the fighter dragons faltered, their flames waning under the assault. With a triumphant roar, five dragons circled above, their glow even more radiant as they continued to blaze a path of protection. Their strong bond for their villagers kept their focus honed on one end. To win.

The enemy dragons were spent, their cool down period had made them vulnerable. The villagers' dragons showed no mercy and seized their moment. The battle was won.

They flew a lap of victory rising higher, uniformly and majestically. The fighter dragons lay below, wounded or dead, no longer a threat.

The sounds of victory from the villagers joined the flapping of the massive wings. A new sound of whooshing and whooping.

Rising higher and higher, as one, the dragons carved graceful arcs through the air. The night breeze ruffled their scales, their wings beat in a synchronized rhythm, and their tails trailed behind them like banners of honour.

The village that had once faced the threat of destruction now witnessed a display of glory and resilience, etching a memory that would be forever ingrained in their collective history. Cheers rang out and embraces were hearty and long. Children ran around or jumped in excitement.

The enemy fire-breathing dragons that had posed a danger were now subdued, their once fiery breaths extinguished. Some lay seriously wounded and no longer able to fight. The threat they had once represented was no more, due to the unwavering determination of the combined villagers and their dragons' bravery.

Amidst the triumphant spectacle in the sky, the sounds of success filled the air. The villagers' cheers and shouts mingled with the powerful flapping of the massive wings above. The once daunting roars of the fighter dragons were replaced by the triumphant sounds - a continuous chorus of whoops, hollers, and exultant cries of joy.

The celebration was not just for the dragons' victory, but for the community that had come together. Heartfelt bonds had been formed from the crisis. There was a closer connection between neighbouring villages and the dragons that had protected their homes..

The dragons had become champions and protectors, and the villagers, once threatened, had been transformed into a broader community. Friendships forged forever.

As the dragons flew home and began to descend, Ridgecliff erupted in jubilation. Handheld flaming torch light illuminated the scene, reflecting a warm glow over the faces of those who had fought and those who had been on the ground. The dragons' wings beat in a triumphant rhythm, their energy glowing. Elation filled the air.

After the dragons had landed among the villagers, the gigantic creatures were embraced. The trial of the fight and shared purpose had brought people and dragons closer together. Victory had only been possible due to the dragons' prowess.

The villagers with the aid of the dragons had triumphed over adversity. The sound of victory echoed from the hearts and voices of all who stood there, united in their celebration of resilience and enduring strength.

The villagers gathered, sharing their personal conquests and recounted how many dragons they had encountered and how many had been killed.

The brothers recounted the details of the battle to their sisters.

Jazintu retreated. She hated listening to these stories of the death of dragons. Inspired by her strong bond with Emeraldesa, she loved all dragons and there was a new feeling growing inside her.

She had felt the rage and fear of her dragon's kin as the fight unfolded. She had doubled over in pain as each enemy dragon was injured. Their wounds became her own, not just emotionally, but physically.

There had to be another way, she thought, one without the suffering and ultimate death of these creatures.

A memory flashed into her mind, a villager striking upwards with a poker-hot sword and a dragon's side being ripped apart. She felt the piercing heat as the weapon was thrust into its side. The pain she felt was as if it was her own, immediate and real. The sensation of hot metal and torn flesh made her feel sick inside. She doubled over momentarily. She could see a massive dragon in her mind's eye as it lurched and fell forward.

It crumpled onto a massive greatsword, piercing deeper into the dragon's body. Then a lightness encompassed her. A floating and disembodied sensation overtook her and she imagined the dragon had died.

Coming back to herself Jazintu screamed, the sound helping to release the pain she had felt. Hot tears welled up and ran down her cheeks. She wiped them away, smudging her face with a dirty hand.

She slumped to the ground and held her head in her hands. This had to stop, the violence and pain should not have to be endured.

Jazintu had kept quiet about her reticence of killing the destructive fire-fighting dragons. What could she say? She could hardly say "don't kill them," when so many people were dying and having their homes destroyed. After all, the dragons were being destructive. Every fibre of her being wanted to stop the death of the dragons but without any alternative she had remained silent. But she believed there must be another way. Perhaps the answers lay with her dragon.

She silently slipped away and returned to her beloved Emeraldesa, still secreted away in the barn.

Chapter 9

Jazintu decided to work harder at observing her own dragon's movements and studying her behaviours. She made a pact with herself to find a solution, to change things so no more dragons would be hurt or killed.

Every day that they flew, she would spend time closely watching Emeraldesa as they soared through the sky, noting the patterns of her flight, the grace of her wings, and the way she adjusted her body in the air. By feeling her movements, watching and learning, Jazintu anticipated what Emeraldesa would do. She learned to adjust her own body to the movements of the dragon so they were like one. Swishing and swooshing, diving and rising, and spiralling at times to land at special places they discovered.

As they glided through the air, she marvelled at the beauty of the world beneath her. The wind whistled past her ears, and the feeling of weightlessness filled her with a sense of wonder. She had become one with the dragon, their destinies intertwined in an exhilarating adventure that would span across the skies.

With every flight, she grew more skilled, navigating the currents and understanding the dragon's silent cues. The dragon became her guide, her protector, and her confidante. Together, they traversed vast landscapes and witnessed breathtaking vistas.

Their trust and friendship grew, showing the power of trust, and the extraordinary bond between a girl and her dragon.
They discovered not only the wonders of flight but also the limitless potential that lay within the depths of their hearts. Her love for Emeraldesa was an ecstatic feeling, unlike any other she had felt before.

She knew they were destined for something epic. There was a purpose to their coming together; she felt sure of it. At night, even in her dreams Jazintu felt connected to her dragon. She would dream she slept with her and some nights she actually did. Jazintu crept out of the house and climbed the barn stairs curling up to her dragon in the loft.

One dream was particularly vivid. She dreamt of a man and his dragon, one that had been in a similar situation to her own. An adult dragon was injured and the man was attempting to help it.

He had medicine that had helped save the lives of those ill in the village. It was a strong concoction of herbs and chillies. In Jazintu's dream he was administering a paste to the sick dragon whilst a young one was by its side. The dragon had a strong reaction and rose up with fiery breath and blew towards the man. He ducked and the flames just missed him. The dragon screamed an horrific loud and high pitched sound, then quite suddenly died.

Jazintu pondered the meaning of this dream. She felt it held a message but wasn't sure what. Perhaps in time it may make more sense if it was indeed a dream of portent, or maybe it *was* simply a dream.

Chapter 10

Jazintu's bond with her dragon was special. She had known for some time that there was more than a bond for each other; a greater purpose was inherent. She started to ponder whether they had a heroic journey to complete. For a while Jazintu had suspected that Emeraldesa was not of a breed she was familiar with. The dragons her brothers flew were a smaller size and their colours differed to hers.

Jazintu knew the dragon she had bonded with was indeed a very different dragon breed.

Emeraldesa was a fire-breathing fighter dragon, likely orphaned by the death of her mother, from the injuries Jazintu had seen. Yet Jazintu realised that her dragon held a key trait. Emeraldesa did not instinctively breathe fire or want to harm her human in any way. Was this due to the gentle love and connection they held?

Jazintu knew this was a significant and somewhat miraculous situation. She had bonded with a fire-fighting dragon and she had not heard of anyone ever doing this. The fire-fighting beasts had long been the enemy of the people of Belongh. They were never usually bonded friends. Those dragons had never before allowed any close contact and never took a rider. Except for Jazintu. This was different; so very very different.

Jazintu began to see a way to help save neighbouring villages from the fighter dragons.
She and Emeraldesa needed to show others how the feared dragons and villagers could live harmoniously. It could be achieved by mutual heart bonding between them. If the villagers and dragons could bond it would avert violence.
With this in mind, she imagined a time without the death of any dragon, no matter what the breed or inclination. Fighter dragons could live alongside both dragons and people keeping their devastating fire traits for other purposes instead of killing people.
That is, if they could be trained to use the fire in other ways. There must be ways to live in harmony, Jazintu mused.

Bonding with dragons was a well-known phenomenon. A bonding can come instantly if the circumstances are right as it had with her and Emeraldesa. She had also heard they could also form more slowly with trust and building up rapport over time. But how to tell the others how to live with an open gentle heart that invited connection, even from the fire-breathing destroyers?
Jazintu realized that in order to save future dragons and villagers from destruction, they needed to find a way to establish a bond with these powerful creatures. If she could do it first, then demonstrate it to others, it would be more likely to succeed.

The secret lay in the fact that Jazintu had bonded with one of the breed that had been senselessly obliterating village after village. She had a seed of an idea. If her dragon could bond with her and protect her, could this be communicated to the other fighter dragons so they too could learn a new way? And as a team perhaps they could help turn the hearts of other dragons to one of protection rather than destruction.

Could the fighter instinct be gradually replaced by an impulse to live with an open, gentle heart with rapport for their humans?

Jazintu had to find out. She jumped onto Emeraldesa's back and they flew to a field near where the fighter dragons had last visited. She saw a few still remained.
Approaching the dragons, she knew they could turn on her in one moment and turn her to ash. But she also knew from the gentle bond with her dragon she could overcome any barrier now, if she just kept an open heart.

Opening her arms wide in a dragon-like manner she bowed her head up and down, then curled her arms in close, like folding wings in. She knelt on the ground and lay forward with her arms like wings folded in, showing what she hoped was vulnerability and surrender. This position being of no threat to the fire
breathing destroyer dragons she hoped it would relay a sense of trust. And it did, her dragon lay next to her in the same position, mimicking her movements and pose.

Esmeralda then lay on her back, showing her belly, a vulnerable act that showed total submission. Could this be enough for the fire-fighter dragons to feel there was no threat? It was a courageous moment for Jazintu and her dragon as they waited helplessly to see what the dragons did next.

Dragons are highly perceptive creatures, capable of sensing emotions and intentions. They approached cautiously, their fiery eyes fixed upon Jazintu. As she lay on the ground, submissively, the fire-breathing destroyer dragons watched her closely.

One of the dragons, the largest and most imposing, took a step forward, its massive wings unfurled and held slightly aloft. It let out a low, rumbling growl, a sound that could easily strike fear into the hearts of lesser beings. However, its body language seemed more curious than aggressive.

A second dragon, slightly smaller than the first, circled around her, maintaining a safe distance. Its movements were fluid and sinuous, its scales glinting in the sunlight. It flicked its tail from side to side, a sign of uncertainty and wariness.

As Jazintu continued to lie there her open-heartedness began to make an impression. The dragons, sensing her lack of hostility, acted curiously. The larger dragon lowered its head, tilting it to the side as if studying her. It emitted a soft, rumbling purr, a deep vibration that reverberated through the air.

The smaller dragon, inspired by the larger dragon's response, cautiously drew closer, keeping its movements slow and deliberate. It raised its head high, its snout nearly touching Emeraldesa. It released a gentle exhale, a warm gust of air, testing scent and intentions.

These actions indicated that the dragons were acknowledging their vulnerability, perceiving both Jazintu and Emeraldesa as non-threatening. They were intrigued by their display of trust and openness.

Esmerelda and Jazintu continued to lie in the same positions. It worked, the dragons' body language transformed from initial wariness to a sense of curiosity and perhaps a hint of trust.

With a bond of understanding beginning to form, the dragons continued their observation, remaining close but still maintaining a respectful distance. They awaited further cues, wanting to ensure that her actions were genuine and consistent.
The dragons' response, while not immediately declaring complete acceptance, conveyed a willingness to explore a potential connection. It was now up to Jazintu to demonstrate her peaceful intentions and build upon the trust that had begun to form.

She slowly stood up, opened her saddle bag and lowered large chunks of goat meat as an offering.
The two dragons leapt on the food, retreating a little to eat it. Smelling the food, more dragons approached until Jazintu and Emeraldesa were surrounded.

Jazintu viewed the landscape of dragons. Their colours seemed to embody the very essence of the environment, each colour telling a story of their origins and the elements they had come to symbolise.

She imagined they were like many other animals or reptiles that over time mimicked some of the background of their environment to better blend with the landscape. An adaptation for species survival perhaps.

There were many of immense stature. As her gaze swept across the scene, she was greeted by a breathtaking display. Each dragon had a unique arrangement of scales that adorned their colossal forms.

The dragons' colours were a masterpiece of nature's palette, ranging from the rich, earthy browns that spoke of ancient forests, to the vibrant and fiery oranges reminiscent of molten lava.

Some dragons boasted scales of deep oceanic blues that held the mysteries of uncharted waters, while others were adorned in regal purples that seemed to emanate an aura of nobility. The colours blended and contrasted with one another, creating a visual symphony that held Jazintu captivated.

But it wasn't just the scales that held this captivating array of colours. As Jazintu observed the dragons more closely, she noticed that each dragon's eyes were a mesmerizing window into their soul. The eyes were windows of irises and pupils that mirrored the same diversity as the scales.

There were gleaming golden orbs that held an eternal wisdom and fierce golden-reds that seemed to burn with determination. The more tranquil green-gold exuded a sense of sagacity. The dragons' eyes held emotions and stories that were beyond words.

Jazintu's admiration deepened as she pondered whether the colours of the dragons were not just a random assortment, but a reflection of the intricate connections between these creatures and the world they inhabited.

As the Sun's rays further illuminated the dragons and painted the scene with an even stronger glow, Jazintu felt a profound sense of gratitude for being able to witness the breathtaking display of colours.
She knew that this experience would forever be etched in her mind, a reminder of the boundless beauty of the dragon world.

Having achieved a visit and not being harmed Jazintu felt confident she could help others now. The dragons she had encountered on the ground appeared to have shifted their attention away from her. She climbed carefully but confidently onto Emeraldesa and they rose and turned swiftly towards home.
Looking behind her she saw that none of the dragons followed her. They rose effortlessly and she leaned into the wind, her hair flowing freely.

Chapter 11

Jazintu needed to devise a plan to demonstrate this power of heart bonding to the villagers and teach them how to establish connections with the destroyer dragons. She could share her success with her brothers and show them what they could do. Once they comprehended, surely they could convey the tactic to the villagers?

Determined to share the incredible discovery of dragon heart bonding with the villagers, Jazintu knew that devising a well-thought-out plan was essential. The power of bonding, even temporarily, held the potential to change the dynamic between the villagers and the feared fighter dragons. It could end all killings. Jazintu devised how she might go about executing her plan.

To begin with she would share her own successful experience with her brothers. As her closest allies, her brothers could provide a supportive and safe environment to demonstrate the newfound connections she had made. Jazintu would let them witness firsthand the transformation in her relationship with the destroyer dragons, showing them that it was indeed possible to establish a bond based on trust and empathy.

Gathering ways to prove it was possible was the key, she told herself. She could gather evidence of the positive changes brought about by the bonding she had experienced. This would include others witnessing the destroyer dragons exhibiting non-threatening behaviours, interacting with other creatures peacefully, or even playing with Jazintu herself. Others seeing how she did would help them believe in her approach.
Then, only then, would there be a chance to save all dragons.

Jazintu and her brothers could jointly present their findings to the villagers. This presentation could take the form of a gathering, a meeting, or a storytelling session. That would depend on each of the various village's traditions. Jazintu's brothers could vouch for the authenticity of her experience and lead the way for the villagers to achieve the same results.

There would be concerns to be addressed. It would be natural for the villagers to be sceptical or hesitant about such a revolutionary idea. Especially when they had experienced harm from the dragons. Jazintu would have to anticipate concerns and questions, addressing them with empathy and patience. Explaining the process, the steps she took, and the potential benefits for both the villagers and the dragons could help allay any doubts.

An actual demonstration for the villagers would be integral. With the support of Jasper and Mordan, Jazintu could arrange a controlled environment with the actual dragons. Seeing what could be achieved would offer hope and a path forward for the villagers. Jasper and Mordan could copy Jazintu's lead, and lie down with the fighter dragons. Then possibly others would have the courage to do the same. By selecting a few willing villagers to participate in the heart bonding process with the destroyer dragons, she was sure that this would allow more villagers to gain confidence in how it was done. They could learn from real life examples. From observation they could experience the transformative power of empathy and trust.

To ensure the villagers would be successful, Jazintu and her brothers would need to offer personal training sessions. That way they would teach the villagers the principles of empathy, patience and respect for the dragons' nature. Slowly they could show them how to approach the fighter dragons with vulnerability that could build trust. It would take time and patience. But it was worth it so that all could live in harmony and, importantly, no more dragons would be injured or die.

Having a plan forming on how to proceed, Jazintu sought her brothers out. The first hurdle was to convince them of her find. Would they even be able to believe that she had found a dragon from another breed? A fire-fighting bred dragon that had adopted her!

Chapter 12

Finding the two just finishing their midday meal, Jazintu joined them at the large kitchen table. "Jasper, Mordan, I have important news," she began.

The brothers turned to her, curious and attentive.

"Oh," said Mordan. "What news do you have, please tell."

"Something unexpected and incredible has happened. I found a dragon," Jazintu announced.

"What, where?" Jasper retorted.

"Well perhaps I should just show you, it's in the old barn," she said. She turned and took a few steps.

"Wait! Just wait a minute Jazintu," Mordan commanded. "We can't simply walk up to an unknown dragon and assume it will be friendly towards us."

Jazintu explained how quickly she had bonded, attempting to reassure them that the dragon was friendly. "I found the baby dragon just before its morning meal. I think this helped with a bond forming.

Its mother had spewed up fish into the cave and I was there when the baby ate."

"That might be so," Jasper retorted, "but how do we know it will be the same with us? Let's get our dragons for protection. Even a young dragon can be fierce. I don't want to get burnt!"

Jazintu took her brothers to the barn, their own massive dragons lumbering closely behind. As Jazintu opened the barn Emeraldesa was sitting in the entrance as if expecting them. Allowing their dragons to approach first, the brothers held back and watched them for their reaction. Both the dragons glanced at Emeraldesa and then lay down in a patch of Sun, stretching out lazily. Seeing their relaxed behaviour the brothers approached the young dragon, holding out a treat of dried fish to help with their first encounter.

Jazintu told Jasper and Mordan how she had come across the young dragon in the cave and how she suspected the mother had died. She described the injuries on the larger dragon and how it failed to return, leaving her to be the one to feed and nurture the young one.

"Jazintu, this is incredible! How did you manage to bond with a dragon? And it is such a magnificent one!"

Jazintu smiled warmly at her brothers' amazement as she shared more of her story. She was eager for them to see for themselves how wonderful Emeraldesa was.

She told them how she had discovered her dragon was of the fire-fighter breed, yet she had still been able to bond by visiting daily at its cave. She explained how it had come to the barn of its own volition.

"Emeraldesa's breed is the fire-fighter breed?" both brothers exclaimed simultaneously.

Jasper was astounded. "It's absolutely amazing that you bonded."

Jazintu responded, "I realise they are mostly known for their fire striking in fighting. Their fire is used to strike and kill other dragons. Yes, it is incredible that I have been able to establish a connection with her, considering their temperament. But it happened!"

"The moment of bonding our eyes met, it was like our souls recognized each other. I extended my hand, and she nuzzled it gently."
"It was a moment of pure magick. From that day forward, Emeraldesa and I have shared an unbreakable bond. We communicate without words," she told them. "As I think of things and match it with images, Emeraldesa gets my message."

As they had entered the barn the emerald-green eyes shone a light that brightened as Jazintu approached. The brothers held back initially as she continued to explain.
"I spent time observing and practicing the mimicking techniques I have seen you two do with your dragons."

She made reassuring clucking sounds to let her dragon know there was no danger from the arrival of her brothers. She imagined hugging her brothers and held this image momentarily. Emeraldesa seemed at ease.
Jazintu explained to Jasper and Mordan how the dragon's connection became so strong. How she had

built on friendly intentions and encouraged trust to flourish. She shared how coming together and playfully exploring energies and activities had become a regular ritual, until they were one and she could ride.

"So, my dear brothers, bonding with a dragon like Emeraldesa isn't just about the breed. Like with all others - it's about patience, understanding and a deep connection that goes beyond the physical world." Jazintu finished her story, her eyes sparkling with the memories of her intimate journey with her dragon.

The brothers were gobsmacked but could tell by certain characteristics of the young dragon that it was in fact of the fire-breathing fighter breed. They kept a healthy distance at first, but reassured by Jazintu's relationship, they patted Emeraldesa. This was accepted and they both were nuzzled by the young dragon.

By involving her brothers and presenting concrete evidence of her success, Jazintu had laid the groundwork for the villagers to embrace the idea of heart bonding with the destroyer dragons. She now hoped she could pave the way for a new era of coexistence between the villagers and these once-feared creatures. Emboldened, she told Jasper and Mordan how she had met with other dragons successfully.

Jazintu provided the details of her adventure, her voice filled with excitement as she recounted a pivotal moment in her journey with Emeraldesa. She explained as their bond grew stronger and how she had felt a calling to befriend the mature fighter dragons.

"To show our intentions and vulnerability, we decided to employ a gesture observed from other animals' behaviours." She went on to explain her special trick.
"We approached the fighter dragons and lay belly up, exposing ourselves - a sign of trust and submission."
Mordan scolded his little sister. "You put yourself at great risk, Jaz!"
"I suppose I did," she replied. "It was a nerve-wracking moment, but I knew it was the only way to convey our peaceful intentions."

"As we lay there, the massive figures of the mature fighter dragons approached us one by one. Their scales shimmered in the light, and they approached us curiously.

Time seemed to stand still as we awaited their response. And then, something incredible happened. One of the fighter dragons, a majestic creature with battle scars and an air of authority, approached us. He nudged Emeraldesa's side with her snout, sniffed and purred. I think it was a gesture of acceptance."

Jazintu continued. "The other fighter dragons followed suit, each of them inspecting us. We had earned their trust through our vulnerability and our shared connection. From that moment on, we seemed to be accepted as allies." She closed her eyes for a moment, remembering.
"It was a humbling experience, my dear brothers, to be embraced by creatures of such power and magnificence. And don't you see how this was such an historic moment. The fighter dragons and I began our mutual

understanding of co-existence. Could this be the start of forging harmony between the dragons and all villagers?"

Jasper and Mordan listened in amazement, hanging on every word of their sister's extraordinary journey with Emeraldesa. Her courage had captivated their hearts, and they seriously wondered if they too could meet the fighter dragons in this peaceful way themselves. But it was a lot to take in. After coming out of the barn the brothers moved apart from Jazintu briefly, consulting on the next move.

Jasper laid out his concerns, "Is this a new way to approach the fighters? Can we take the same risks as Jazintu, or will the others still strike with fire, as our own dragons are fighters now too?"
Mordan, ever the more practical said, "It is a consideration, but we can't risk all our friendly dragons' lives at once. If we try this we must do a controlled approach with just a few dragons."

Chapter 13

Mordan and Jasper gathered the villagers and explained their sister's new plan. Jazintu began by sharing her own experiences of bonding with the baby dragon, highlighting the moments of instant connection and the gradual growth of their relationship through patience and compassion. She emphasized that it was crucial to approach the destroyer dragons with an open mind, without judgment or fear.

To demonstrate their point, Jazintu showed the villagers drawings of her dragon and one of the destroyer dragons, with both displaying calmness and respect. A record of her interactions with the fire fighter dragons showed her proximity to them and remaining safe. Images portrayed her supine position, and others depicted her sharing food with her own dragon and the bigger ones.

She explained that by appearing vulnerable and using submissive body language she had shown the dragons that she was not a threat to them. Confidence was built through this non-threatening behaviour which was a communication method all dragons understood. She went on to tell them how she and Emeraldesa had been able to establish a friendly connection that allowed her to be safe and not harmed by the fire fighter dragons in any way.

"Actions speak louder than words," she said. And she went on to explain how sharing food was a universal act that instinctively helped alleviate any remaining reticence the dragons might have held.

Jazintu suggested to the villagers that her brothers mimic what she had done. "Jasper and Mordan can do it with some dragons and can come back and report how it went for them. If they're successful it will prove that anyone can befriend the dragons. The goal will be to end years of living under the threat and fear of destruction once and for all."

"Then, if you are brave enough, we can find some fighter dragons and many more of us can do it together." She lay on the ground like a dog laying down for a belly rub. "Like this!" She laughed. "It may be as simple as copying me and getting your dragons to do it too."

Jasper and Mordan showed they were willing to take up the challenge. They lay on their backs and giggled as they pawed the air in gentle play. Standing again, the brothers announced to the gathered villagers that they would like to do it. There were murmurs amongst those gathered and a few in a small group began discussing the idea.

"Can it be done?" one of the elders began.
"It's a brave idea and not one without risks," Elvsbreath mused.
Her son, Guyzam, volunteered. "I shall go with them and assist."
Knowing her son's strong mind, she didn't argue. "Alright son, but take care, armour up and take longswords."

"There is no time to waste," Jasper announced.

And cupping his hands around his mouth Jasper called his dragon, "Whizzardree, Wizz, Wizzarrrr!" He made a long low whistle.

Mordan followed suit and called his dragon to him also, "Thaumaturge, "Thaw, Thaw," he bellowed. The sky darkened directly above them and two massive dragons flapped heavily above, squawking and cooing.

They signalled for them to land and signalled to them to lie on their backs. Both dragons rolled over and the humans hurriedly moved aside to allow enough space. The dragons' claws flailed the air gently and they half-closed their eyes in friendly demeanour. Their thick leathery scales were now exposed with a thinner underbelly skin. The posture made them prone to be easily killed. Uncomfortable, the dragons' breath was laboured but they briefly lay still to show complete surrender.

"Up, up!" the boys commanded. The pair quickly rolled and raised themselves, glad to be upright once more.

Jazintu applauded them and approached Wizzardree and stroked him as he bowed his head to reach down to her. She moved over to Thaumaturge and stroked his neck. Both blew warm breath and her hair flew back from the hot stream of air. She laughed and turned to her brothers. "Are you ready to find fighter dragons and do this for real?"
Jazintu leapt onto Emeraldesa and looked down for her brother's response.

Nodding, the brothers climbed onto their rides bareback, Guyzam with his swords behind Mordan. In gloved hands they all held onto raised scales, and leant forward. The brothers clicked their dragons into flight, with Jazintu and Emeraldesa in the lead. Flying a safe distance behind her, Mordan and Jasper flew in formation, wing tip to wing tip gliding at the same height, just slightly above their sister. Below them, Emeraldesa's jade shiny scales glinted in the Sun and Jazintu's red cloak floated out creating a majestic artwork.

Jazintu let out a gleeful screech and the brothers whooped in reply. The brothers' dragons were blue and turquoise. Emeraldesa, shimmered silver, gold and green. Her exquisite colours added ethereal beauty to the aerial tableau. The sunlight played on her wings, creating a mesmerizing display of light and shadow.

The brothers communicated through subtle gestures and shared glances; a silent language born out of their time together. Mordan and Jasper's trust in each other was unwavering, evident in the synchronized movements of their flight. They navigated the currents effortlessly. Guyzam was flying a short distance behind the trio, his dragon flying with ease in the slipstream of the others.

As they continued their journey, the world below unfolded like a living tapestry. Mountains, rivers, and forests sprawled beneath them. They traversed with ease the vastness of the realm they explored. The four flew on, the thrill of their adventure fuelling their spirits as they soared towards the horizon. Far off to the west there was a dark cloud in the sky, a cloud that flickered with filtering light. Light that was made by the flapping of many wings.

A huge group of dragons was traversing the sky in unison so that the shroud of bodies created a dark mass visible in the distance. The 'cloud' grew bigger as the fighter dragons came closer. They were heading directly towards a village on the lower slopes of the island. Jasper, Mordan and Jazintu turned towards it, their smaller, faster dragons bound to reach the village before the thunder of fighter dragons.
Once they were close to the village, the four landed, hidden by a small ridge.

They alighted and discussed their plans. Mordan began, "As we agreed, when the first scout fire-fighter dragon approaches the village, it's then that one of us will approach." "And that has to be me," said Jazintu. "I have to be the one to build on the trust with a few fighter dragons to begin with. Your dragons can follow suit and show more of the others, once we have one or two that have befriended me." The others agreed, knowing the Jazintu had already had success, so it made sense to follow her lead.

The sky blackened overhead, the mass of dragons temporarily blocking out the Sun. Flapping wings in large numbers made a deafening sound as the thunder landed. Under disguise of the noise Jazintu leaped into action. Without hesitation, she urged her dragon into flight, swooped over the ridge and landed at the foot of the first dragon she spied. Jumping off, she gave Emeraldesa the command to surrender. The young dragon swiftly obeyed, rolled onto her back and pawed the air. Jazintu lay beside her and did the same. A loud screech filled the air as the massive dragon was surprised by their presence. Jazintu froze, awaiting the outcome of her valorous actions.

The massive maroon dragon turned its head towards the small dragon at its feet, then sniffed at Jazintu. Steam snorted from its nostrils and Jazintu felt the warmth touch her body, penetrating her thick flying garb. She cooed encouragingly, pulled out some dried goat meat and threw it in the direction of the dragon's head that loomed above her.

Hungry from its long flight, the maroon-coloured dragon licked up the morsel, throwing its head back as it swallowed. A happy purr-roar rang out with satisfaction and the dragon visibly relaxed its posture, its huge legs half-sitting, so that the dragon sat down with half its body lying on one side. Jazintu threw more strips of meat forward and before it could be all taken too quickly signalled to her brothers to join her.

Jazintu fed Emeraldesa a precious piece of goat's cheese, one of her favourite treats, and the dragon immediately let out her own loud purr-roar that rang out for all to hear. The unmistakable sound from the younger dragon reached Mordan and Jasper who were ready to join the bonding challenge. Arriving one behind the other, they signalled their dragons to land beside two fighter dragons. Each with their own dragon to befriend, they alighted and lay on their backs alongside their dragons. Giving the coo-coo command and slapping their sides Wizzadree and Thaumaturge took the instruction and lay supine with their bellies exposed.

Guyzam had copied the others and a fourth dragon was delighting in the meat offered as both Guyzam and his dragon lay prone in their vulnerable positions. Having been fed, all the dragons who had snorted and fumed and roared, now lay relaxed and offered no threat towards any of them.

Every aspect of the drill had worked, the ploy was a success. Not waiting too long to test the theory on the whole thunder, the four retreated swiftly. Dropping the last of their goat's meat to distract the dragon valour team flew off. They were keen to return home to share their accomplishment with those eagerly awaiting the news.

The four dragons swept into the central yard of Ridgecliff, landing in unison. The villagers hurried to them astutely aware that the outcome was crucial to their future lives. Jasper proclaimed victory, "Jazintu's valiant plan was a success, her efforts prevailed. She is to be applauded, all of us were able to tame the fighters."

Guyzam confirmed it, announcing confidently, "They are right, it worked on the few we approached. We should be able to return home safely once we roll out the behaviour to the larger thunder of dragons."

The villagers were astounded and shared their musings, "Could this really be the solution, could this end the dragon wars?"

The villagers started to comprehend the possible consequences of this approach. They realized that by undertaking the same tasks with bravery and in large numbers they too could befriend the fire fighter dragons. Peace may prevail.

By cultivating trust, even the most ferocious adversaries could be approached with the intention of creating harmony rather than being a part of perpetual conflict and destruction.

Inspired by the example set by Jazintu, her dragon, the two brothers and Guyzam, the villagers embraced the concept. The principles of heart bonding were able to be replicated, intentionally and consciously. The power of living with an open, gentle heart offered a new era in the way they lived. Future generations would no longer live in fear of attacks from fighter dragons. Loud cheers rang out across the compound. Those close to Guyzam, Jazintu and her brothers clasped them and hugged them hard.

They thanked them and told them they were ready to start interacting with the fighter dragons. It was time to befriend them instead of living in fear, under the threats of constant aggression and violence.

The brothers began discussing when more could be taken to meet the fighter dragons. They agreed that the villagers would join in, and they would take turns in flying them in. There was a flurry of activity as bags were being packed with provisions and riders ran to put on their leathers for flying.

Chapter 14

The leather saddle bags were filled with an assortment of food, enough to sustain the riders and their dragon companions throughout the journey. Fruits, dried meats, bread, and water skins were carefully packed, ensuring that everyone had enough sustenance for the trip.

To ward off the chill of the open skies, woven and woollen wraps were chosen to keep an additional layer for the riders' warmth. These wraps were not only practical but were a traditional style, befitting the classic design of their outfits. The villagers took pride in their appearance, embracing their connection to the dragons with a nod to the past.

As the villagers prepared for their journey to neighbouring villages, excitement filled the air. The bonds between humans and dragons had grown stronger, and this expedition was history in the making. A way to showcase their peaceful coexistence to fighter dragons. The preparations were meticulous, ensuring both the comfort and safety of the riders and dragons.

Until the fighter dragons had attacked the village, swords had primarily been used for dress purposes. The villagers' training in medieval sword fighting had allowed them to add a glamorous addition to their attire.
The swords served as a reminder of their ancestors and their dedication to protect and uphold their values. They had rarely been used in battle.

Many of the villagers with older and larger dragons adorned their majestic companions with decorative neck and flank garb. These ornate embellishments created a regal look to the dragons' appearance, showcasing their uniqueness and beauty. Some riders wore dress swords for the occasion.

With provisions gathered and everyone complete with their armour, the villagers and dragons were ready for their journey. The air crackled with anticipation as the group set off, eager to introduce their harmonious bond to neighbouring villages and expand the circle of connection between humans and dragons.

It had started with one brave act by Jazintu, but one they felt they all had to do. The survival of their village and others in the land had relied on this success. Peace would reign and they could live without fear and rebuild their lives.

The sky filled with dragons and riders. Fire breathing and swashbuckling would be for sport and not war. It was the cusp of a great era and one that would be told in tales in front of hearth fires for many generations to come.

Two scouts on smaller faster flyers went ahead to locate some fire-breathing fighter dragons. After flying to the site, a group of about 20 dragons and riders swept down to land.

The fire-fighter dragons were laying in the ashes of burnt trees and logs, some rolling in it and others sweeping ash onto their backs with their massive wings.

As the group landed the ash covered dragons rose up and a flurry of black air briefly drifted up with them. The scene looked ominous, but undeterred the villagers landed and leapt down beside their mounts.

Mordan, Jasper and Guyzam began the befriending method, commanding their dragons to roll on their backs with their bellies in the air. Unrolling a food wrap, goat's meat was held out towards the dragon closest to them. A deep blue muzzle sniffed, then lifted its head into the air and blew a huge stream of fire. The flame held blue, red and orange streaks. The brothers were surprised the food was not immediately taken. Were they about to be attacked? They signalled to the villagers behind them to retreat and withdrew several metres to a safer distance. What was wrong? Why didn't the food get taken?

Jazintu, who had started to withdraw with the others, turned and watched as her brothers tried to coax the blue dragon. A roar and more flames caused her to turn and go to her brother's aid. The three men were pulling back, and they tried to stop Jazintu. "It's too dangerous sis!" Jasper insisted. Emeraldesa was following beside Jazintu as, undaunted, she continued her approach.

"There, there, my beauty," she cooed. The blue dragon turned its steely grey eyes on her and took a deep breath as if to fuel for a fire shot. Emeraldesa overtook Jazintu and scuttled under the blue's head. Lifting her turquoise nose, she sniffed and let out a long "eeeep" followed by another louder, "EEEEP." The blue exhaled a little and nuzzled the young dragon.

Mordan got out a more bloodied piece of meat and threw it towards the dragon. A huge sneeze with snot and ash erupted from the massive dragon. Then it leapt on the meat, swallowed and looked around for more. Perhaps its nose and sense of smell had been impeded by the ash, and Emeraldesa had provided some reassurance, but all seemed well now. A couple of other dragons ambled towards them.

Jasper signalled for the group to return, and many paired off with food to commune with the dragons. Other sneezes were heard and the brothers laughed with relief as the danger of a failed exercise now seemed over. As the villagers offered food and subsequently stroked those they tamed, their confidence increased and more repeated the pattern until many of the once-feared dragons were won over.

There were many valiant trips to bond additional villages where there were still dragons on the ground. Gradually villagers and fighter dragons developed a symbiotic relationship. The gift of food and submissive positions were the initial catalyst to change. But the intent of befriending the fearsome ones seemed to then take over. Both parties quickly recognised a friendship and a helper in the other. The food had been important and the body language had also been vital. But it was the intent to befriend that had won out.

The fighter dragons, no longer feeling threatened or marginalised, became protectors rather than destroyers. Mordan and Jasper envisaged how they could use their fire-breathing abilities for positive purposes, such as clearing land for cultivation or deterring other threats to the village. Their newly made human friends would feed them and help care for them in return. A new era had begun.

Through their heroic journey with dragon valour and the power of mutual heart bonding, Jazintu had paved the way to save many villages from the fire-breathing destroyer dragons. She had transformed the entire dynamic between humans and dragons across the island. Their example served as a lesson that with an open, gentle heart, even the most formidable barriers can be overcome.

The dragon riders' swords that were used in battle were now once more worn only for decoration. More time was now spent on repairs to their outfits and the creation of new garb to be worn for comfort and appearance, not as armour in war.

The riders' outfits were donned in pride only as commemoration of their days of valour. There was no need for fighting anymore.

Peace reigned, villages flourished. On leisure days dragons filled the sky with riders, and dragons without riders flew in unison alongside them.

Fire-breathing dragons were no longer a beacon of terror, but they were nevertheless monumental, their massive bodies a stunning sight to see. Magnificent, their flaming breath that had been so terrifying to behold was no longer a danger or threat to the villagers. But was it all over? What had caused the dragons to turn on the villagers and kill so many without any apparent provocation.

Could this truly be the start of a long era of peace, or was it only a temporary situation? Jazintu wondered if she could discover what had triggered the dragons' violent and destructive nature.

"Sure, flame throwing and killing was instinctive to them," she mused, "but what had caused them to fly into villages and senselessly kill?" Maybe she would fly over the lands that had been affected, talk to people and do research, gather stories and see if she could shed light on the situation.

But for now, it was time to enjoy the newfound peace. She set off to find her family and plan a celebratory feast. She found some mead and sat down with her siblings and raised a toast.

"To our dragon's success and to Emeraldesa for showing the way," she declared.

"To Emeraldesa," her siblings gleefully shouted, "and to you Jazintu," they announced, raising their mugs together.

Taking deep draughts of their drinks and laughing heartily, they were relieved the fights were over and the days of senseless destruction were at an end. Plans were underway for rebuilding villages but for tonight it was a time for feasting and fun.

They celebrated their dragon valour well into the night, other villagers joining them and making merry with song and dance around the camp fire. Huzzah!